How Do You Make a Baby Smile?

BY Philemon Sturges

Illustrated by Bridget Strevens-Marzo

HarperCollinsPublishers

For Mother Earth's children —P.S.

To Doug Cushman with thanks for
his encouragement —B.S.M.

How Do You Make a Baby Smile?
Text copyright © 2007 by The Estate of Philemon Sturges
Illustrations copyright © 2007 by Bridget Strevens-Marzo.
Manufactured in China. All rights reserved. No part of this book may be used or
reproduced in any manner whatsoever without written permission except in the case
of brief quotations embodied in critical articles and reviews. For information address
HarperCollins Children's Books, a division of HarperCollins Publishers, 1350 Avenue
of the Americas, New York, NY 10019.
www.harpercollinschildrens.com

Library of Congress Cataloging-in-Publication Data is available.
ISBN-10: 0-06-076072-9 (trade bdg.) — ISBN-13: 978-0-06-076072-4 (trade bdg.)
ISBN-10: 0-06-076073-7 (lib. bdg.) — ISBN-13: 978-0-06-076073-1 (lib. bdg.)

Typography by Stephanie Bart-Horvath
1 2 3 4 5 6 7 8 9 10 ❖ First Edition

How do you make a baby smile?
Grin like Papa Crocodile,

Or, like Mama Elephant,
wiggle your ear,

Or shake your horns
like Daddy Deer.

How do you make
a baby laugh?

Twist your neck like
Papa Giraffe,

Or make a face

like Mama Baboon,

Or play peekaboo
like Daddy Raccoon.

How do you make a baby coo?
Sing like Daddy Robins do,

Or, like Mama Chickens, cluck all day,

Or, like Papa Crickets,
fiddle away.

So how do you make a baby grin?
Tickle the baby under its chin!

When baby yawns
and nods its head,

Tuck the baby snug in bed.